Sky-High Sukkah

by Rachel Ornstein Packer

illustrated by Deborah Zemke

APPLES & HONEY PRESS

Springfield NJ • Jerusalem

To Larry—you're my heart, my home, my sukkah
To Leah and Ari, my real-life inspirations
— RP

For Phoebe
— DZ

Apples & Honey Press
An imprint of Behrman House and Gefen Publishing House
Behrman House, 11 Edison Place, Springfield, New Jersey 07081
Gefen Publishing House Ltd., 6 Hatzvi Street, Jerusalem 94386, Israel
www.applesandhoneypress.com

ISBN 978-1-68115-513-5

Library of Congress Cataloging-in-Publication Data

Names: Packer, Rachel Ornstein, author. | Zemke, Deborah, illustrator.
Title: Sky-high Sukkah / by Rachel Ornstein Packer ; illustrated by Deborah
Zemke.
Description: Springfield, New Jersey : Apples & Honey Press, [2016] |
Summary: Leah and Ari build a Sukkah on Ari's rooftop and the neighbors
get together to help decorate it and everyone enjoys the Sukkot
holiday together.
Identifiers: LCCN 2015035551 | ISBN 9781681155135
Subjects: | CYAC: Sukkah--Fiction. | Sukkot--Fiction. | Jews--Fiction. |
Neighbors--Fiction.
Classification: LCC PZ7.1.P27 Sk 2016 | DDC [E]--dc23
LC record available at http://lccn.loc.gov/2015035551

Design by David Neuhaus/NeuStudio
Edited by Dena Neusner
Printed in China
1 3 5 7 9 8 6 4 2

Leah lived high up in an apartment building overlooking the busy world below. In the early morning, she would gaze out her window and watch the sun bathe the city in a soft, golden light.

Today, however, the city was pearly gray, and Leah felt just as sad as the weather. Sukkot was coming, and Leah had no place to build a sukkah. There wasn't any backyard, and no one was ever allowed up on the apartment roof. This meant that she had to go somewhere else to celebrate the holiday.

As Leah was walking to school, she made her usual
stop at Al's fruit market. She liked the way everything
looked so colorful, and Al was always happy to
see her.
He was outside spraying misty water
on the neat rows of fruit, making them
look like precious, sparkling gems. Leah
stood quietly, watching him.

"You look a little sad today," Al said.

"I was just thinking that these fruits would look pretty hanging in a sukkah." Leah sighed.

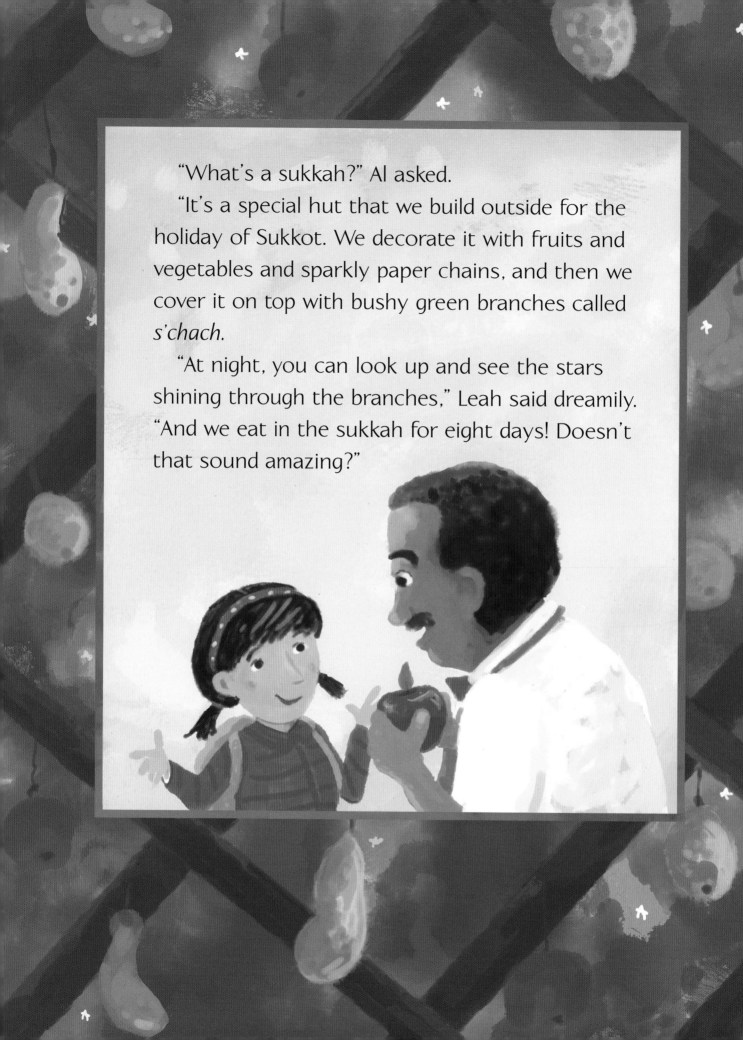

"What's a sukkah?" Al asked.

"It's a special hut that we build outside for the holiday of Sukkot. We decorate it with fruits and vegetables and sparkly paper chains, and then we cover it on top with bushy green branches called s'chach.

"At night, you can look up and see the stars shining through the branches," Leah said dreamily. "And we eat in the sukkah for eight days! Doesn't that sound amazing?"

"Yes," Al agreed. "So why are you so sad?"
"We have no place to build it," Leah replied.
Just then, Leah's best friend, Ari, ran up to her.

"Check out my newest drawing," he said. The jagged buildings and rooftops reminded Leah of a giant jigsaw puzzle.

"The view from my roof was awesome." Ari flipped to the next drawing.

"Look, Al, I even drew your fruit store." Ari carefully ripped out the page and handed it to him.

"This is terrific!" Al said.

Leah pointed at the next picture. "Al, that's a sukkah," she said.

"It looks just the way you described it, Leah. Do you have one, Ari?"

"No." Ari shook his head. "I've always wanted one, and our roof is the perfect place for it, but my mom and dad say that a sukkah costs too much money."

Later, Leah and Ari heard an announcement at Hebrew school about a Sukkot poster contest. The prize would be a real sukkah! Ari looked over at Leah and whispered, "This is our chance!"

"I can't," Leah said. "I have no place to put a sukkah. In our building, no one is *ever* allowed up on the roof."

"Don't worry," said Ari. "If I win, we'll build it on my roof, and we can share it!"

"Thanks." Leah smiled, although she still wished she could have a sukkah of her own.

Ari spent the rest of the day working on his poster. He painted a city skyscraper with a sukkah at the tippy top, bursting with leafy branches and colorful fruits and vegetables.

When Leah saw the poster, she said, "You should call it *Sky-High Sukkah!*"

Ari liked the title so much, he wrote it across the top.

Sunday was contest day, and time seemed to tick backward as Leah and Ari waited to hear who would win.

When classes were over, the principal finally announced, "The winner of the contest is . . . Ari Freed."

"I can't believe it!" Ari shouted. "Come on, Leah, we have a sukkah to build!"

Leah and Ari were eagerly making plans to eat in the sukkah every day when Leah's mother picked them up after school.

"I can't wait to tell my mom and dad," Ari said.

"We're meeting them at Al's, so you can tell them your good news then." Leah's mother smiled.

Ari raced over to his parents.

"I have a surprise—I won the sukkah poster contest at Hebrew school!" Ari shouted.

"That's terrific!" Ari's mother exclaimed.

"The prize was a real sukkah. So now we can build it on the roof! Isn't that great?"

"Yes, but . . . I'm afraid we can't accept it," Ari's father said sadly.

"Why not?" cried Ari.

"Because we didn't plan for it. Our storage space is just too small, and there's no room in our apartment to store all the sukkah pieces. I'm really, really sorry."

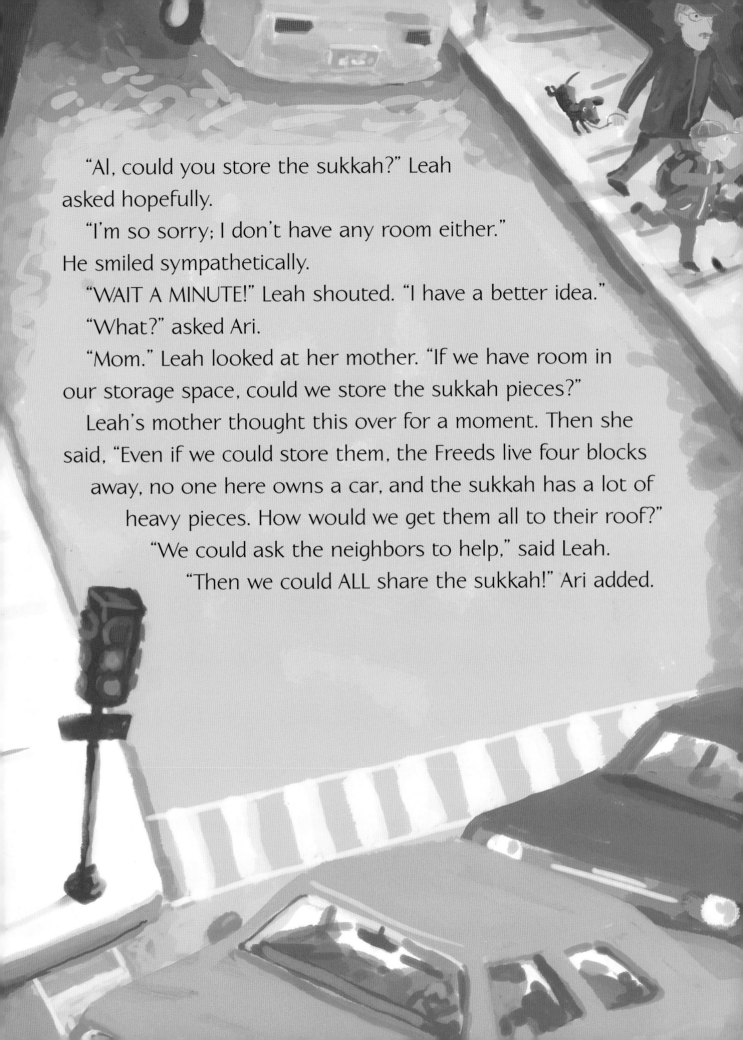

"Al, could you store the sukkah?" Leah asked hopefully.

"I'm so sorry; I don't have any room either." He smiled sympathetically.

"WAIT A MINUTE!" Leah shouted. "I have a better idea."

"What?" asked Ari.

"Mom." Leah looked at her mother. "If we have room in our storage space, could we store the sukkah pieces?"

Leah's mother thought this over for a moment. Then she said, "Even if we could store them, the Freeds live four blocks away, no one here owns a car, and the sukkah has a lot of heavy pieces. How would we get them all to their roof?"

"We could ask the neighbors to help," said Leah.

"Then we could ALL share the sukkah!" Ari added.

When the news got out about the sukkah, lots of people volunteered to help.

Some offered to build it. Others agreed to organize a special Sukkot dinner.

Leah and Ari worked on paper chains to string on top and hang on the walls.

Their moms bought some greens for the roof.

Finally, the sukkah was finished—just in time for the holiday. Leah and Ari hung their paper chains and stepped back to admire their work. But something was wrong.

"It doesn't look anything like my *Sky-High Sukkah* poster," said Ari, shaking his head.

"You're right. It looks . . . empty." Leah sighed.

"I thought there would be way more branches," Ari added.

"And there aren't any hanging fruits or vegetables. The paper chains are pretty, but the sukkah looks boring without anything else," she said.

"Well, at least we have a sukkah," Ari remarked.

"You're right, Ari," Leah agreed.

Just before sunset on Sukkot, the neighbors' excited chatter and laughter echoed through the hallways as they made their way up to the roof. Once they reached the sukkah, however, their chatter stopped.

Everyone stared at the sukkah in amazement.

It was spilling over with bright-green bushy *s'chach* that smelled wonderfully spicy, and it was bursting with glossy vegetables and colorful fruits— and there was Al standing inside! Leah watched as he placed a large basket of crisp apples on the table.

"Now that's more like it!" Ari declared.

"Al! Did you do all this?" Leah asked.

"I knew you were disappointed when you couldn't have a sukkah of your own," Al said, "so I wanted to help make this one extra special."

Leah smiled. It was truly a neighborhood sukkah. She listened to her neighbors chatting as they got things ready for dinner. She breathed in the fresh scent of *s'chach* and looked up through the branches at the pinkish evening sky. She knew the stars would be out soon.

"You know what, Al?" Leah said.

"What?"

"This is SO MUCH better than a sukkah of my own!"

Dear Friends,

When I was growing up in Queens, New York, my family had a small wooden sukkah on the back porch where my brothers and I would happily squeeze ourselves in between our parents and other assorted guests. My neighborhood friends would come over for snacks as we cozily sat inside eating candy corn and apples. I loved that for eight days, lots of different people were in and out of our sukkah all the time. Truthfully, I was always a little sad when we had to take it down.

Being part of a community is an important Jewish value. This is called *kehilla* in Hebrew. Why do you think it is so important to have a *kehilla*? Who are some of the people in your *kehilla*?

Building a sukkah is a great opportunity to invite people over, but what happens after we take it down? What other activities can you do to build a strong *kehilla*?

Have a fun, sukkah-tastic holiday.

Rachel